LEARN TO

DETECTIVE DAN

and the

Missing Marble Mystery

written and illustrated by

Timothy Roland

ZondervanPublishingHouse
Grand Rapids, Michigan
A Division of HarperCollinsPublishers

Detective Dan and the Missing Marble Mystery
Copyright © 1993 by Timothy Roland

Requests for information should be addressed to:
Zondervan Publishing House
Grand Rapids, Michigan 49530

Library of Congress Cataloging-in-Publication Data

Roland, Timothy.
    Detective Dan and the missing marble mystery / Timothy Roland.
      p. cm.
    Summary: With the help of his Bible, Detective Dan solves the case
of his friend Tara's missing marbles.
    ISBN 0-310-38091-X (pbk.)
    [1. Greed—Fiction. 2. Conduct of life—Fiction. 3. Christian
life—Fiction. 4. Mystery and detective stories.] I. Title.
PZ7.R6433Df   1993
[E]–dc20   93-3495
                                                     CIP
                                                     AC

Edited by Dave Lambert and Leslie Kimmelman
Interior and cover design by Steven M. Scott
Illustrations by Timothy Roland

Printed in the United States of America

93 94 95 96 97 98 / CH / 10 9 8 7 6 5 4 3 2 1

For Mom and Dad,
who helped me become
a Bible Detective

CONTENTS

Chapter One
MISSING MARBLES

I am Detective Dan.

I like to solve mysteries.

I also like to read.

One day I was reading my Bible.

I looked at my verse for the week.

Watch out! Be on your guard against all kinds of greed: Luke 12:15

What does that mean? I wondered.

Just then the doorbell rang.

It was Tara.

She was acting crazy.

"I lost my marbles," she said.

"You have to help me find them."

Good! I, Detective Dan,

had a case to solve.

"How many marbles
are you missing?" I asked.

"Three," said Tara. "All of them red."

"Where did you last see them?"
I asked.

"Come, I will show you," Tara said.

I got my detective things.

I followed Tara.

Newton, my dog, followed me.

We soon met our friend Bernard.

He was not playing

with marbles.

He was playing with a ball.

The ball had a bell inside.

"Did you lose your marbles too?"

I asked.

"No," said Bernard.

"I traded them to Tara

for this cat ball."

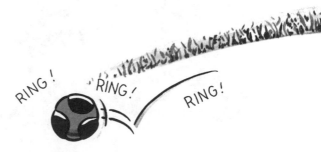

RING! RING! RING!

"It belonged to Scratch," said Tara.

Scratch was Tara's cat.

I did not ask any more questions.

I was afraid of Scratch.

So was Newton.

I followed Tara to her house.

She opened the door.

Newton would not go in.

I did not want to go in either.

But I had no choice.

I was on a case.

Tara's brother, Jasper,

was pushing a toy truck.

He pushed it right over my foot.

The truck was heavy.

And it rattled.

Jasper laughed.

But I, Detective Dan, did not
think it was funny.

Chapter Two
THE MARBLE QUEEN

We went to Tara's room.

"Here's where it happened,"
she said.

I looked into the room.

I saw a pile of marbles.

A great big pile.

Sitting next to the marbles was
Tara's cat, Scratch.

"You have lots of marbles," I said.

"I know," said Tara. "And they're
all mine! Mine! Mine!"

"But why do you need them?"
I asked.

"Need them?" said Tara.

"I don't need them. I *want* them.
I want all the marbles!"

I looked at Tara.

Then I thought about my verse
for the week. *Be on your guard
against all kinds of greed.*
Tara did not guard against greed.
And now she was very greedy.

Tara climbed onto her pile
of marbles like
a greedy marble queen. "If I had all
the marbles,"
said Tara, "no one could play
marbles without me."
I wanted to leave.
I do not like people who are greedy.
But I did not leave.
Because I, Detective Dan, was
on a case.

"How many marbles are there?"

I asked.

"Not enough," said Tara.

"There should be 743 marbles.

But there are only 740."

"How do you know?" I asked Tara.

"I counted them," she answered.

"Maybe you counted wrong," I said.

"Let's count them again."

I moved toward the pile.

Scratch moved toward me.

She showed me her claws.

I moved back.

"Scratch is my guard," said Tara.

"Isn't she good?"

I shook my head.

I did not have to shake my knees.

They were already shaking.

Tara put Scratch out of the room.

We counted the marbles.

There were 739.

"Four are missing," I said.

"Oh, no!" cried Tara.

"Someone stole another marble!
But how?
Scratch was guarding the door."

"Maybe a thief came in
another way," I said.
I looked around the room.
The window was open.
"Maybe someone climbed
in the window," I said.

"I don't think so," said Tara.
"That would have been too noisy."
"Nonsense," I said.

I walked to the window.

I wanted to show Tara how quietly
someone could climb in.

I climbed out the window.

I stepped down.

"Ouch!"

I climbed back in.

I pulled stickers out of my coat.

"You're right," I said.

"Coming through the window
is too noisy."

Tara laughed.

I did not.

Chapter Three
MARBLES AND MICE

I opened the bedroom door,

looking in the hallway for clues.

Scratch walked in.

"Maybe the thief got past Scratch,"

I said.

"How?" asked Tara.

I looked at Scratch.

She raised her claws in the air.

I hid behind Tara.

"No one can get past Scratch,"

said Tara.

"Except me.

And my

brother."

I looked at Tara.

"That's it!" I said.

I walked to the living room.

I picked up Jasper's toy truck
and shook it.

Something inside rattled.

"I, Detective Dan, have
solved your case," I said.

"So where are my marbles?"
asked Tara.

"Inside this," I said.

I held up the toy truck.

Jasper jumped
up and down.

"Mine! Mine! Mine!"
he yelled.

"I'm ashamed of
you, Jasper," said Tara. "Where did
you learn to behave like that?"

I looked at Tara.

But I said nothing.

I just opened the toy truck's door.

Stones and dirt fell out

onto my sneakers.

Being a detective is sometimes

a dirty job.

Newton and I headed home.

As I passed a fence I heard a noise.

It sounded like someone playing

with marbles.

I looked through

a hole in the fence.

I was right.

It was the sound of marbles.

Four marbles, to be exact.

And all of them were red.

Farley was playing with them.

Next to him was his slingshot.

I had to be careful.

Newton agreed.

I ran to Tara's house
to tell her what I had seen.
She grabbed a bag.
She followed me back to the fence
and looked through the hole.
"Are those your marbles?" I asked.
"No," said Tara. "My red marbles
don't have stripes on them."
"Then this was
a waste of time," I said.

"No it wasn't," said Tara,

"because Farley has nice marbles.

I want them. And I will get them."

She climbed over the fence.

I climbed after her.

Newton watched through the hole.

"I want your marbles," said Tara.

Farley stood up.

He crossed his arms.

He stepped forward.

I stepped back.

"You can't have them," he said.

"Not even for this?" asked Tara.

She pulled something from her bag.

It was a windup toy mouse.

Farley looked
at the toy.
He handed his
marbles to Tara.
She smiled.

Farley wound up the mouse.

It moved across the field.

Farley shot it
with his slingshot.
He smiled.
Everyone was
happy.

Except Scratch. She had lost a toy.

And me. I still had a case to solve.

And I had run out of clues.

Chapter Four
MARBLE TOYS

Newton and I walked slowly home.

I tried to think.

But my stomach

was growling too loudly.

So I ate a banana.

I gave Newton a dog biscuit.

Then I read my verse for the week.

"Watch out! Be on your guard

against all kinds of greed."

 I thought about greed.
It makes people
want what they
really don't need.
Sometimes it even makes
people do bad things.
I was guarding
against greed.
Tara was not.
The only thing

she was guarding was her marbles.

 I lifted my head.
That was it!
That was the clue
I needed to solve
my case.

35

Newton and I rushed to Tara's house.

He stayed outside. I went in.

Tara was counting her marbles.

Scratch was guarding them.

"Bad news," said Tara.

"Someone stole another marble."

"I, Detective Dan, know who it was,"

I said.

"You said that before," said Tara.

"But this time I'm right," I said.

I led Tara into the hall.

We hid in a closet.

"What are we doing?" asked Tara.

"Watch and see," I said.

We peeked out the door.

Soon we heard a marble.

It rolled out of Tara's room.

Behind the marble was Scratch.

She was pushing it

toward the back door.

"Scratch is the robber!" said Tara.

"Shh!" I said. "She may lead us

to the other missing marbles."

Scratch pushed the marble

out the cat door.

She pushed it into the bushes.

Tara and I followed quietly.

There were the missing marbles.

Scratch was playing with them.

"Scratch!" scolded Tara.
"You are a bad cat!
Why did you take my marbles!"
"Maybe she needed something
to play with," I said.
"She can play with her toys,"
said Tara.

"What toys?"
I asked.
"You traded them
all away
for marbles."

"Oops," said Tara.
"I never thought of that."
"I did," I said.

"And that was the
key to this case.
You forgot about
your guard."

"You mean Scratch?" asked Tara.
"Yes," I said. "But you also forgot
something else.
You forgot to guard against greed.
And greed caused your problem."

Tara took her marbles inside.

I followed. So did Scratch.

"Thanks for solving my case,"
said Tara. "As a reward,
I will let you play marbles with me."

"I don't want to play marbles,"
I said. "I want to play catch
with Newton."

"Then what should I do
with my marbles?"
"Trade them back
for Scratch's toys," I said.
Scratch smiled.
I think I made a friend.
But I did not stay to find out.

Newton and I went home.

We played catch.

I ran, and he tried to catch me.

I was glad I could finally play.

Solving this case had been
hard work.
But no case was too hard
for Detective Dan.

THE
MISSING MARBLE MYSTERY
WRAP-UP REPORT

VERSE FOR THE WEEK:

"Watch out! Be on your guard

against all kinds of greed."

Luke 12:15

THE CULPRIT: GREED

Greed is when you want more

than you need.

QUESTIONS FOR DETECTIVES:

✔ Who was greedy in the case of the missing marbles?

✔ What greedy things did she do?

✔ What problems did her greed cause?

✔ What does the Bible say about greed?

✔ Have you ever been greedy?

✔ When?

✔ What happened?

CONCLUSIONS:

✔ God doesn't want us to be greedy.

✔ Greed is the cause of lots of trouble.

✔ Guard against greed!

CASE CLOSED

Detective Dan